Little Fox Goes to the End of the World

By Ann Tompert

Illustrated by Laura J. Bryant

Marshall Cavendish Children

To Lord Larry and Lady Gay Beetlebaum
—A.T.

To Bruce
—L.J.B

Text copyright © 1976 by Ann Tompert
Illustrations copyright © 2010 by Laura J. Bryant
Marshall Cavendish Corporation, 99 White Plains Road, Tarrytown, NY 10591
www.marshallcavendish.us/kids
Library of Congress Cataloging-in-Publication Data
Tompert, Ann.
Little Fox goes to the end of the world / by Ann Tompert ; illustrated by
Laura J. Bryant. — 1st ed.
p. cm.
Originally published by Crown Publishers in 1976, with illustrations by
John C. Wallner.
Summary: Little Fox tells her mother all the frightening things she will
see and do when she travels to the end of the world.
ISBN 978-0-7614-5703-9
[1. Voyages and travels—Fiction. 2. Imagination—Fiction. 3. Mother and
child—Fiction. 4. Foxes—Fiction.] I. Bryant, Laura J., ill. II. Title.
PZ7.T598Li 2010
[E]—dc22
2009046009

The illustrations are rendered in watercolor on Strathmore bristol paper.

Book design by Anahid Hamparian

Editor: Margery Cuyler

Printed in Malaysia (T)
First edition
1 3 5 6 4 2

Little Fox was chasing a butterfly. Her mother sat nearby, sewing her a new jacket. Farther and farther Little Fox strayed.

"Come back, Little Fox," called her mother, "or you may get lost."

Little Fox walked back to her mother ever so slowly. She was tired of playing in the soft, green grass near the mouth of her den.

"Some day," she said, "I'm going to travel to the end of the world."

"Oh," said her mother, "is the end of the world very far?"

"Yes," said Little Fox. "It is very, very far. I will have to go through a deep forest to get to it."

"Won't you get lost?" asked her mother.

"Oh, no," said Little Fox. "I will carry a lantern."

"What will you see?" asked her mother.

"Bears!" exclaimed Little Fox.

"Oh, dear!" cried her mother, dropping the jacket and covering her eyes. "Won't you be scared?"

"No," laughed Little Fox. "I like bears. I'll take a pot of honey along and give some to each bear I meet."

"That's a good idea," said her mother. "I would not have thought of that. What else will you see?"

"Tigers!" shouted Little Fox. "They will roar and growl and try to scare me!"

"I'd hide," exclaimed her mother.

"Not me," said Little Fox. "I'll take my drum and I'll beat it as loud as I can. I'll scare THEM away!"

"I'm glad," said her mother.

"But the noise will scare the elephants. They will come charging after me."

"I'd be scared," said her mother.

"Not me," said Little Fox. "I'll take a ladder so I can climb up a tree."

"You will be safe there," said her mother.

"No, I won't," said Little Fox. "There will be monkeys in the tree and they won't like my being there."

"Oh, my goodness!" said her mother.

"Don't worry," said Little Fox. "I'll take some bananas. They will like that."

"Is the end of the world in the forest?" asked her mother.

"Oh, no," laughed Little Fox. "I will have to leave the forest and cross the mountains. They will be covered with snow."

"Will it be hard?" asked her mother.

"Yes," said Little Fox. "And the snow will be deep. The icy winds will try to freeze me."

Little Fox's mother shivered and wrapped her shawl around her shoulders.

"But I'll run like the wind," said Little Fox.

"And you will have your jacket to keep you warm," said her mother, as she put it on Little Fox to see how it would fit. "Then will you be at the end of the world?"

"No," said Little Fox. "I will have to cross the hot desert, but I'll take Father's old umbrella to protect me from the sun."

"Then will you be at the end of the world?" asked her mother.

"Oh, no," said Little Fox. "I will have to cross a river filled with crocodiles. They'll be waiting to gobble me up." Little Fox's mother gasped.

"Don't worry," said Little Fox. "I'll take my boat and, if you lend me your broom, I'll sweep the crocodiles out of my way and sail down the river to the open sea."

"You will be safe then," said her mother.

"Only if I may borrow your clothesline and four pillowcases," said Little Fox.

"What for?" asked her mother.

"To make a lasso and capture the Four Winds. Then I will put each wind in a separate bag."

"But how will you sail with no wind?" asked her mother.

"I'll let the East Wind out. It will fill my sails and send me toward the end of the world," said Little Fox.

"That will be nice," said her mother.

"Oh, no, it won't. The East Wind will blow up a storm. It will rock and roll my boat and try to smash it against the rocks."

Little Fox's mother threw her apron over her head.

"But I'll let the West Wind out," said Little Fox. "It will blow my boat away from the rocks."

"Good," said her mother. "You will be safe then."

"No, I won't," said Little Fox. "It will blow me into the island of the One-eyed Cats."

"That sounds awful!" cried her mother. "What will you do?"

"I'll let the South Wind out," said Little Fox. "Its gentle breeze will blow me to the end of the world."

"At last," said her mother.

She put on Little Fox's jacket and buttoned it up. "But I shall miss you."

"And I shall miss you," said Little Fox. "So I'll let out the North Wind and head straight for home."

"And I shall be waiting for you with your favorite dinner," said her mother.